BULLYSAUKUS
THE GLADIATOR

Damon Burnard

Hodder
Children's
Books

a division of Hodder Headline

For my mother,
Mary, with love

Copyright © 1997 Damon Burnard

First published in Great Britain in 1997
by Hodder Children's Books

The right of Damon Burnard to be identified as the Author and Illustrator of the Work has
been asserted by him in accordance with the Copyright, Designs and Patents Act 1988.

10 9 8 7 6 5

A Catalogue record for this book is available from the British Library

ISBN 0 340 68979 X

Printed and bound in Great Britain by
The Guernsey Press Co. Ltd, Guernsey, Channel Islands

Hodder Children's Books
A Division of Hodder Headline plc
338 Euston Road
London NW1 3BH

Once upon a time, in a forest, on an island, in a swampy, steamy sea, there lived a bunch of dinosaurs in happy harmony . . .

CHAPTER ONE

Bullysaurus - also known as
Grill'o'Saurus - loved to cook.
One day he was strolling through
the forest, looking for exciting new
ingredients, when something caught
his eye.

It was a great bird, winging its way
across the sky.

All of a sudden, Bullysaurus didn't feel like looking for exciting new ingredients any more.

He stumbled over to a tree, sat down and let out a big, sad sigh. The bird reminded Bully of a terrible thing that had happened long ago.

CHAPTER TWO

When Bullysaurus was younger, he lived on the other side of the forest with his brother.

They were always up to something or other. They'd go diving in the lake.

Play hide-and-seek in the jungle.

Or explore the slumbering volcano.

One day, they came upon a huge tree. It was so tall, you couldn't even see its top branches.

And off they went, scrambling up the trunk as fast as they could.

Bully's brother took the lead. When Bully got to the top, he was waiting.

"Look at THIS!" he shouted.
He was standing in a huge nest, next to a humungous egg.

"Be careful!" warned Bullysaurus.

"Oh, phooey!" his brother scoffed.
"I bet she's miles away!"
But she wasn't. In fact, she was
very close indeed.

The bird's wings beat like thunder as she raced back to her nest.

"LOOK OUT!" yelled Bully.

SHE'S COMING!

But it was too late. Down she dived, sweeping up Bully's brother . . .

Eek!

. . . and carrying him off in her terrible talons!

Bullysaurus fled back down the tree. When he reached the ground he looked up at the sky. The bird was no more than a distant speck . . .

Then even the speck disappeared, and Bully never saw his brother again.

CHAPTER THREE

Thinking about his brother made
Bullysaurus sad . . .

. . . so he decided not to. He was
about to get up from the tree,
when . . .

. . . down fell a massive net . . .

. . . and Bullysaurus was trapped!

The more he struggled, the more entangled he became. And then . . .

. . . out from the bushes jumped a group of strange, two-legged creatures, covered all over with hair!

They surrounded Bullysaurus,
whooping and dancing for joy!

Bullysaurus tugged and tore at the
net, but it was no use. Finally, he
could bear it no longer.

Out snorted great balls of fire,
scattering the creatures, sending
them diving into the bushes.

All except one.

"Excellent!" said the creature, who wore a crown on his head.

From his robe he took a hollow reed and, putting it to his lips, he blew.

Bullysaurus felt a prick in his side.

All of a sudden he felt very
drowsy, and before he knew it . . .

. . . he was fast asleep!

CHAPTER FOUR

When Bullysaurus woke up, he found
himself lashed to the mast of a ship.
He was headed for a strange island.

The creature in the crown
approached his prisoner.

"Who are you?" Bully asked.

said the King of the Nuks.

"Please!" begged Bully. "Please set me free."

"I'm afraid that's not possible," the king replied carelessly.

"But you'll get your chance for freedom soon enough . . ."

CHAPTER FIVE

The ship docked at last.

Bullysaurus was marched across a gangplank . . .

. . . and pushed into a huge cage.

The king stood triumphantly on
top, while a dozen Nuks pulled Bully
through the steets of a cave-man
town. The cave-men were everywhere.

They lined the streets, crowded
the buildings and hung from the
trees. They cheered and roared as
Bully passed by.

When the procession reached the
mouth of a great cave, Bully was
wheeled inside.

"You'll find out soon enough!"
cackled the king. Then he clicked his
fingers, and in walked a big Nuk,
bearing a vast pot of food.

"Now, eat!" demanded the king, as the Nuk pushed food at Bully through the bars of the cage.

In vain Bully fought to be free, and when he tried to snort fire, he found that his pilot-light had been snuffed out!

The king rubbed his hands with delight.

"That's it!" he crowed.

CHAPTER SIX

And so the days passed in that
gloomy cave, and Bullysaurus began
to lose hope of ever seeing his
friends or his home again.

Every day the king would prod and
torment him, and when Bully
snapped and snarled, he would
dance around with glee.

YIPPEE!

Three times a day the big Nuk visited, each time carrying a bigger pot of food.

One day, when Bully refused to eat, the Nuk wagged a finger at him.

"Tsk!" tsked the Nuk, as if Bullysaurus had just asked the stupidest question ever.

"The fight tomorrow!" said the
Nuk wearily. "Against the Gladiator
of the Unks."

said the Nuk.
"Why are they bad?" asked Bully.

So it went on, with Bully asking
questions, and the impatient Nuk
answering them, more or less.

And this is what Bullysaurus found
out . . .

CHAPTER SEVEN

Bullysaurus was a captive on an island that looked something like this:

Diagram One

The island was inhabited by two tribes of two-legged creatures, the Nuks and the Unks:

Fur

No fur

A Nuk   An Unk

Diagram Two

As you can see, the main difference between them was that Nuks are covered with hair, and Unks are not. For this reason, the Nuks and the Unks called each other names.

The name-calling turned into fighting . . .

. . . the fighting turned into a war.

One day the King of the Nuks and the King of the Unks agreed that enough was enough.

And so they decided to divide the island in two:

Diagram Three

The Nuks lived on the left-hand side, and the Unks on the right, so they'd never have to see each other again.

But one day a problem arose. And the problem looked something like this:

Diagram Four: what the problem looked like...

On the border dividing them, there stood a tree, on which there grew the biggest, juiciest apples you've ever seen. Of course, the Nuks and the Unks wanted these all to themselves.

Before long they were fighting over who the apples belonged to.

Each tribe dug a trench on either side of the tree. That way, they could make sure the other tribe didn't pick the apples.

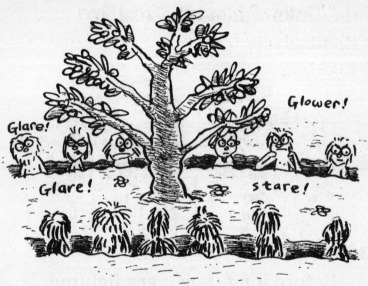

And all the while, the tree grew . . .

One day, the kings met. Neither wanted to go to war again, but they had to decide who should have the apples. The Nuk king had an idea.

"I know," he said. "You find a gladiator, and we'll find a gladiator, and they'll fight instead of us!"

So it was agreed.

And now the contest was about to take place. Guess who was gladiator for the Nuks?

CHAPTER EIGHT

The next morning, in strode the king. "Prepare yourself, Beast!" he declared.

A dozen Nuks led Bullysaurus out of the cave and through the town.

On they went, until at last they came to a great meteor crater.

Bullysaurus and the king stood at its centre, while the tribe of Nuks took their seats on its steep sides.

They all turned their eyes to a distant dust-cloud drawing nearer and nearer.

Towards them marched the Unk tribe who, headed by their king, were pulling along a huge covered cage.

The cage was rolled into the middle of the arena, and the Unks took their places, across from the Nuks.

"So," sneered the Unk king.

The Unk king laughed.
"Then this will be a very quick
fight!" he jeered, and he tore the
covering from his cage.

CHAPTER NINE

Inside stood the most ferocious
beast that Bullysaurus had ever seen!

"Tsk!" sniffed the Nuk King, trying
to sound unimpressed.

"The tree to the winning tribe!" said the Unk king.

And with that decided, the kings took their seats.

The gladiators stood face to face,
toe to toe, under the blazing sun.

"Listen!" whispered Bully.

"Me neither," boomed
his opponent.

And he hurled himself at
Bullysaurus.

Bullysaurus struck back . . .

The battle raged!

The Unk champion hit the ground
hard, and off flew his helmet.

But Bullysaurus froze.
"Oh my goodness!" he gasped.

CHAPTER TEN

It was true! The gladiator was none other than Bully's brother; the brother he thought he'd never see again!

The blood-thirsty crowd was
growing impatient.

The gladiators each took a wild swing . . .

. . . and dropped to the ground . . .

. . . at EXACTLY the same time!

"Your gladiator fell before mine!"
snapped the King of the Unks.

Before you knew it, the Unks and the Nuks were arguing ferociously about who was the victor!

Quietly, Bully and his brother got to their feet.

They were tippy-toeing out of the arena, when suddenly . . .

Under cover of a great cloud of smoke, Bully and his brother ran away as fast as they could . . .

CHAPTER ELEVEN

Off they raced, down to the shore, the angry Nuks and Unks at their heels.

They leapt on board a raft . . .

. . . and left the ranting and raging cavemen hopping on the shore!

When the Nuk king calmed down (which took quite a while) he said a very strange thing.

"They've shown us that more can be achieved by working together than by fighting!" he said.

59

CHAPTER TWELVE

Over the ocean drifted the brothers, into the unknown.

Bully's brother talked about his life; his escape from the giant bird, his amazing travels and adventures, and finally his capture by the Unks.

And all the while the sun blazed down, until their lips were dried and cracked.

Of land there was not a speck in sight. They began to fear for their lives.

Suddenly, Bullysaurus heard a familiar voice.

Bully looked up into the sky.

Since his disappearance, Bully's friends had searched high and low and near and far, but were losing hope of seeing him ever again. How happy they were, when Terry steered Bully and his brother safely home!

They hugged and laughed, and hugged some more, and then Bully told them all about his long-lost brother.

"What a wonderful, delightful, amazing day!" gushed Theo, and everyone agreed.

"C'mon!" laughed Delores.

In silver moonbeams and soft starlight
The dinosaurs danced with great delight,
Until once more the sky turned blue,
And the emerald forest shone with dew . . .